· LINDA MAYBARDUK ·

JAMES
the Dancing Dog

ILLUSTRATED BY GILLIAN JOHNSON

TUNDRA BOOKS

To James and his parents, Joanne Nisbet and David Scott —
To my children and the Growly and Ivy —
And to all the furry creatures I have loved.

— L.M.

To Linda Robinson

— G.J.

Text copyright © 2004 by Linda Maybarduk
Illustrations copyright © 2004 by Gillian Johnson

Published in Canada by Tundra Books,
481 University Avenue, Toronto, Ontario M5G 2E9

Published in the United States by Tundra Books of Northern New York,
P.O. Box 1030, Plattsburgh, New York 12901

Library of Congress Control Number: 2004100839

National Library of Canada Cataloguing in Publication

Maybarduk, Linda
    James the dancing dog / Linda Maybarduk ; illustrated by Gillian Johnson.

For ages 3-8.
ISBN 0-88776-619-6

    I. Johnson, Gillian II. Title.

PS8626.A93J34 2004   jC813'.6   C2004-900493-X

We acknowledge the financial support of the Government of Canada through the Book Publishing Industry Development Program (BPIDP) and that of the Government of Ontario through the Ontario Media Development Corporation's Ontario Book Initiative. We further acknowledge the support of the Canada Council for the Arts and the Ontario Arts Council for our publishing program.

Medium: watercolor and ink on paper
Design: Kong Njo

Printed in Singapore

1 2 3 4 5 6   09 08 07 06 05 04

Once, not so many years ago, the National Ballet of Canada had:

  1   director
 55 dancers
  5   teachers and coaches
  3   pianists
  2   conductors
 45 musicians
 15 crew members and . . .
  1   extraordinary dog.

From the very first day, Puppy James went everywhere with his new mom and dad — even to their work at the ballet company. James loved being in the studio.

Dancers are a very special breed, he thought to himself. *I'm going to be just like them.*

James got right to work. He practiced his pliés and jumps
along with the dancers.

"Look!" said his dad. "I think James is taking class."

"Of course he is," answered his mom. "Isn't he adorable?"

All the dancers clapped and shouted, "Good boy, James."

James felt right at home.

By the time he was a little older, James had taken on several responsibilities.

In class he helped his mom and dad teach.

During rehearsal he bravely helped the male dancers perfect their lifts.

And at lunchtime he helped everyone by making sure they stayed in trim dancing form. It was a busy life, but James was the dog for the job.

James kept busy at the theater, too. Before every performance the dancers gave his tummy a rub for good luck.

But James wanted to be more than a good luck charm. He longed to dance on the stage, too!

Night after night, he watched from the wings as the dancers performed their magic. He dreamed of following them into the spotlight.

But they always said, "Stay here, James, old buddy. You don't belong onstage."

James refused to give up. He worked
doggedly to improve.

He grew taller and lost his puppy
fat, but even so, his dancer's soul stayed
wrapped in a beagley body.

One day James heard a commotion out in the hall. The dancers were crowded around the bulletin board. "How exciting!" one of them said. "We're going to dance *Giselle*!"

"Look, James!" called another. "It has a part for a hunting dog."

A hunting dog! That will be me, James thought, wagging his tail.

On the first morning of rehearsal, James bounded into the studio
with his dad. There, in the middle of the room, stood a tall,
long-legged wolfhound. James growled.

"Why is this wolfhound here?" his dad asked the choreographer.

"He's our hunting dog!" the choreographer replied. "Isn't he
wonderful? He has all the elegance and majesty we need for a
ballet like *Giselle*."

What they really *need is a dog who can dance like me,* sniffed James
to himself. Heartbroken, he crept behind the piano.

"We will begin with the
hunt scene," shouted
the choreographer.
"Bring the wolfhound
in with the hunting party."
James felt worse with
every passing minute.

He watched in disgust.
The wolfhound just sat
there. He did nothing
with his role. What sort
of hunting dog neither
sniffed nor snuffed, trailed
nor tracked, posed nor
pointed? James ached
with disappointment.
If only he had the chance,
he knew exactly how
he would play the part.

On opening night, there was the usual backstage hustle and bustle.

Dancers warmed up.

Stagehands prepared the props.

Wardrobe people fiddled and
fussed with the costumes.

The wolfhound was led to the wings.

"Onstage, please!" shouted
the stage manager.

"Where is James?" asked
the dancers. They wanted
to give his tummy a good
luck rub.

But all James wanted to
do was hide.

When the hunting bugle blared, the wolfhound walked elegantly onto the stage just as he had during rehearsals. But in rehearsals there had been no bright lights, no loud music, and no huge sea of faces.

The terrified dog took one look at the audience and jumped into the dancer's arms. Stage fright had struck.

From his hiding place James heard some muffled chuckling when there shouldn't have been any. *Strange,* he thought. James couldn't help himself. He stole a peek.

Just then the wolfhound scrambled down and bolted offstage. Horrified, the dancers whispered, "Now what are we going to do?"

The audience roared with laughter.

I know exactly what to do, said James to himself.

Picking up each paw he pranced nobly, taking his rightful place onstage.

For a moment the lights dazzled him, but then his training took over.

Spinning in small spirals, he sniffed and snuffed.

He posed and pointed at his prey.

Then he sprang into a soaring grand jeté and found himself
just where he had always dreamed of being . . .

. . . in the spotlight at center stage.

Bravo, James!